A Note to Parents and Caregivers:

With a focus on math, science, and social studies, *Read-it!* Readers support both the learning of content information and the extension of more complex reading skills. They encourage the development of problem-solving skills that help children expand their thinking.

 The PURPLE LEVEL presents basic topics and objects using high frequency words and simple language patterns.

 The RED LEVEL presents familiar topics using common words and repeating sentence patterns.

 The BLUE LEVEL presents new ideas using a larger vocabulary and varied sentence structure.

 The YELLOW LEVEL presents more challenging ideas, a broad vocabulary, and wide variety in sentence structure.

 The GREEN LEVEL presents more complex ideas, an extended vocabulary range, and expanded language structures.

 The ORANGE LEVEL presents a wide range of ideas and concepts using challenging vocabulary and complex language structures.

When sharing a content focused book with your child, read to find out facts and concepts, pausing often to restate and talk about the new information. The realistic story format provides an opportunity to talk about the language used, and to learn about reading to problem-solve for information. Encourage children to measure, make maps, and consider other situations that allow them to apply what they are learning.

There is no right or wrong way to share books with children. Find time to read and share new learning with your child, and pass on the legacy of literacy.

Adria F. Klein, Ph.D.
Professor Emeritus
California State University
San Bernardino, California

Editor: Christianne Jones
Designers: Hilary Wacholz and Amy Muehlenhardt
Page Production: Michelle Biedscheid
Art Director: Nathan Gassman
The illustrations in this book were created with acrylics.

Picture Window Books
5115 Excelsior Boulevard
Suite 232
Minneapolis, MN 55416
877-845-8392
www.picturewindowbooks.com

Printed in the United States of America.

Library of Congress Cataloging-in-Publication Data
Aboff, Marcie.
The lemonade standoff / by Marcie Aboff ; Illustrated by Troy Olin.
p. cm. — (Read-it! readers. Math)
ISBN-13: 978-1-4048-3668-6 (library binding)
ISBN-10: 1-4048-3668-3 (library binding)
1. Arithmetic—Juvenile literature. 2. Addition—Juvenile literature. 3. Money—
Juvenile literature. 4. Competition—Juvenile literature. 5. Fairness—Juvenile
literature. I. Olin, Troy, ill. II. Title.
QA115.A26 2008
513.2'11—dc22   2007004015

The Lemonade Standoff

by Marcie Aboff
illustrated by Troy Olin

Special thanks to our advisers for their expertise:

Stuart Farm, M.Ed.
Mathematics Lecturer, University of North Dakota
Grand Forks, North Dakota

Adria F. Klein, Ph.D.
Professor Emeritus, California State University
San Bernardino, California

PiCTURE WiNDOW BOOKS
Minneapolis, Minnesota

It was a hot summer day. Jen and her friends sat on Jen's front stoop.

"I'm bored," said Jen.

"I'm thirsty," said Katy.

"Let's go upstairs and get some lemonade," said Jen. "Maybe we'll think of something to do."

Jen's brother, Nick, was drinking a cup of pink lemonade.

"I like pink lemonade," said Katy.

"I like yellow lemonade better," said Jen.

"Me, too," said Sam.

"Hey, I have an idea! Let's have a lemonade stand," Jen said.

"Let's sell pink lemonade," Nick said.
"More people like yellow," Jen said.
"No, they don't," said Nick.
"Yes, they do," said Jen.

"Let's have a contest," said Jen. "Sam and I will sell yellow lemonade. You and Katy can sell pink."

"I'll bet we'll sell more," said Nick.

"I'll bet we will," said Sam.

"If I win, you have to clean my room for a week," said Jen.

"If I win, you have to clean MY room for a week," said Nick.

"Let the games begin," said Katy.

Jen's mom helped them make two big pitchers of lemonade. One pitcher had yellow lemonade. The other pitcher had pink lemonade. Then Jen took out lots of plastic cups.

They set up a table in front of their apartment building. Just then, Mrs. Miller walked by.

"Hi, Mrs. Miller!" said Jen. "Would you like some cold yellow lemonade?"

"How about a cup of frosty pink lemonade?" asked Katy.

"Lemonade sounds great," said Mrs. Miller. "I'll have a cup of the yellow."

"All right!" said Sam. "We sold the first cup!"

LEMONADE FOR SALE

A man from the building next door stopped by the lemonade stand.

"I'd like a cup of lemonade," he said.

"Would you like pink lemonade?" asked Katy.

"No, thank you," said the man. "I'll have a cup of yellow lemonade."

"It's two to zero," said Sam.

1 + 1 = 2

Mrs. Jones came by with her two children. She and her daughter wanted pink lemonade, and her son wanted yellow.

MONADE FOR SALE

Jen and Nick's mom came to check on the lemonade stand.

"How many cups have you sold?" she asked.

"We've sold three cups of yellow lemonade," said Jen.

"We've sold two pink so far," said Katy.

Nick whispered something in Katy's ear. She laughed. "Good idea!" Katy said.

LEMONADE FOR S

Yellow Pink
III   II

Nick ran upstairs. He came downstairs with a plate of cookies. He taped another sign in front of the table. It read, "Free Cookie with Pink Lemonade."

"That's not fair!" cried Jen.
"You can't do that!" said Sam.

Twins John and Jane stopped by the lemonade stand.

"What a deal," said John. "Those cookies look good! I'll buy one cup of pink lemonade."

"I'll buy two cups of pink lemonade," said Jane. "Coming right up!" Katy said.

1 + 2 = 3

Nick counted. "We already sold two lemonades, and we just sold three more. Two plus three equals five," he said. "We're leading!"

"I know what we can do," Jen said and then whispered something to Sam.

"Great idea!" he said. "Let's do it!"

Jen ran upstairs. She came back holding a cooler with Popsicles inside. Jen hung a big sign on the table. It read, "Free Popsicle with Yellow Lemonade."

"Now people can really cool off!" said Sam.

Jen's mom called the children in for lunch.

"How many cups have you sold this morning?" she asked.

Jen and Sam sold twelve cups of yellow lemonade during the first hour. They sold ten cups during the second hour.

"That's a sum of twenty-two cups," Mom said.

12 + 10 = 22

Katy and Nick sold ten cups of pink lemonade during the first hour. They sold thirteen cups during the second hour.

"And that's a sum of twenty-three cups," Mom said. "It looks like the pink team is ahead."

10
+ 13
―――
23

After lunch, the kids from summer camp walked by on their way to the park.

Jen and Sam sold twelve more cups of yellow lemonade.

22

+ 12

____

34

Nick and Katy sold eleven more cups of pink lemonade. Both teams had a sum of thirty-four. They were tied!

23 + 11 = 34

Jen's mom came downstairs.

"Time to wash up, Jen and Nick," she said.

"Oh, Mom, not yet," cried Jen. "We need to sell one more lemonade to break the tie."

Just then, Jen saw her neighbor Mr. Lee walking toward the table.

"Mr. Lee," she called out. "Have some lemonade—some yellow lemonade!"

"No, no," Nick called out. "You will like the pink better."

"My goodness," said Mr. Lee. "I like both flavors, but I don't want two cups of lemonade."

"I think I'll have the yellow," he said.
"Yeah!" said Jen. "We won!"
A big smile spread across Sam's face.
He poured the yellow lemonade for Mr. Lee.

"Wait," said Mr. Lee. He held up his hand. "That's enough."

"But it's only half a cup," said Jen.

"Yes, I know," said Mr. Lee as he took the cup and put it in front of Nick and Katy. "Please add some pink lemonade to my cup."

"Yeah!" said Katy.

Nick grinned. He poured the pink lemonade to the top of the cup.

Mr. Lee tasted the lemonade mix.
"That's the best lemonade I've ever had!"
he said. Mr. Lee started to walk upstairs.

"Mr. Lee," Jen called out. "Don't forget your
cookie and Popsicle."

"Do I get half of each?" Mr. Lee asked.

"No, you can have a full cookie and a full Popsicle," she said. "After all, you made up a whole new drink flavor: yellow-pink lemonade."

"Excuse me," said Katy. "It should be called pink-yellow lemonade."

"But we poured the yellow lemonade first," said Sam.

"It doesn't matter," said Jen. "I have the perfect name for the new lemonade."

"What is it?" Nick asked.

"Orange lemonade," she said.

With that, everyone smiled and agreed that the lemonade standoff would remain a tie.

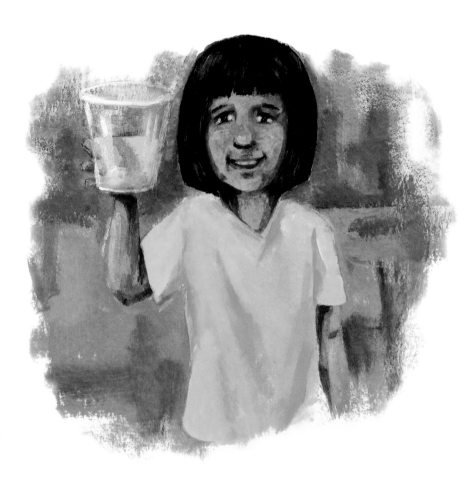

34 + 34 = 68

Addition Activity

Jen, Nick, Katy, and Sam sold a total of sixty-eight cups of lemonade. Grab a piece of paper and a pencil and add up the problems below. Which team sells more in each problem— the pink team or the yellow team?

1. $14 + 12 = ?$

   $10 + 11 = ?$

2. $44 + 32 = ?$

   $52 + 34 = ?$

3. $25 + 14 = ?$

   $31 + 15 = ?$

4. $73 + 15 = ?$

   $24 + 65 = ?$

Glossary

add—to find the sum of two or more numbers
equals—being the same in amount
plus—with the addition of
sum—the number you get when you add two or more numbers together

To Learn More

At the Library

Cleary, Brian P. *The Mission of Addition*. Minneapolis: Millbrook Press, 2005.

DeRubertis, Barbara. *A Collection for Kate*. New York: Kane Press, 1999.

Gisler, David. *Addition Annie*. New York: Children's Press, 2002.

Leedy, Loreen. *Mission—Addition*. New York: Holiday House, 1997.

On the Web

FactHound offers a safe, fun way to find Web sites related to this book. All of the sites on FactHound have been researched by our staff.

1. Visit *www.facthound.com*
2. Type in this special code: 1404836683
3. Click on the FETCH IT button.

Your trusty FactHound will fetch the best sites for you!

Look for all of the books in the *Read-it!* Readers: Math series:

The Lemonade Standoff (math: two-digit addition without regrouping)
Mike's Mystery (math: two-digit subtraction without regrouping)
The Pizza Palace (math: fractions)
The Tallest Snowman (math: measurements)